Bod's Mum's Knickers

"Watch out! Don't lose them!" Bod's mum gave a great leap and grabbed the trailing edge of her speeding knickers. "Relax, I'm in control!"

But Bod's mum spoke too soon, for the fish were pulling hard.

They dragged her under. *"Wha-hoah!"* Bod's mother yelled.

"Yah-hey!" she cried again as her round head bobbed back up.

We all covered our eyes as the net reached the edge of a high waterfall.

PETER BEERE

Bod's Mum's Knickers

Illustrated by Philip Hopman

For Hanni and May

Scholastic Children's Books,
Scholastic Publications Ltd,
7–9 Pratt Street, London NW1 0AE, UK

Scholastic Inc.,
555 Broadway, New York, NY 10012-3999, USA

Scholastic Canada Ltd,
123 Newkirk Road, Richmond Hill,
Ontario, Canada L4C 3G5

Ashton Scholastic Pty Ltd,
P O Box 579, Gosford, New South Wales,
Australia

Ashton Scholastic Ltd,
Private Bag 94407, Greenmount, Auckland,
New Zealand

Published by Scholastic Publications Ltd, 1995

Text copyright © Peter Beere, 1995
Illustrations copyright © Philip Hopman, 1995

ISBN 0 590 55832 3

Typeset by Contour Typesetters, Southall, London
Printed by Cox & Wyman Ltd, Reading, Berks

10 9 8 7 6 5 4 3 2 1

Chapter 1

At the end of our lane, where the fields meet the tarmac, is the house where my friend lives with his weird family.

Theirs is a big house with roses round the door, and a washing line outside that looks like solid steel. It needs to be that thick because three times a week it copes with washing day.

Bod's mum does a big load, and I don't just mean "big". She does a load so big it could break most folks' arms. The biggest part of all is Bod's mum's huge knickers. They are gigantic.

Those knickers bother me. They're *fantastic* – they're as big as parachutes. When the wind makes them flap they crack like thunder. They make our cat take off like every dog in town is after it.

I once wrote to someone at the RAF, suggesting that they could use those knickers as jet-plane air brakes. But my mother saw my note and made me tear it up.

I really think you could use them as air brakes, though; you could send them up as kites or cut-price weather balloons.

It's hard to believe that anyone on earth could be big enough to wear them.

Bod's mum works at our school – Frimley

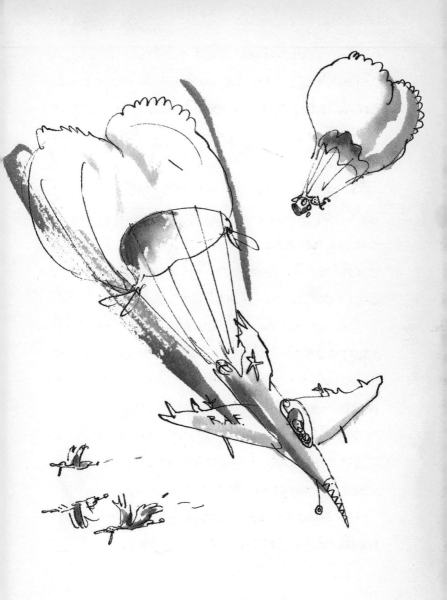

School. She's our dinner lady. This is probably a good job, as she really likes her food, and loves to sample it before she hands it out.

But Bod's mother isn't fat; she's gone way beyond fat. She's ENORMOUS. She's a very nice lady who always makes me laugh. She's kind of round and soft, like dough. She has thick curly hair, and wears bright, jolly clothes covered with flowers and things.

She's a really good mum, and I'd like her for my own. Well, no; I like my mum more than I like Bod's mum. But she's still pretty good. As far as mothers go, she's up there near the top.

It's her knickers which really bother me; those knickers she hangs out on the washing line. Clean ones every day. Two damp pairs on the line, cracking like thunder.

Chapter 2

About the end of June our town caught the tail end of an Atlantic hurricane. It was mostly out at sea, but Britain caught its heel and got kicked in the teeth. Storms thundered through our land like teams of wild horses, galloping out of control.

The storms snatched up houses, and threw cars around like toys. They ripped down

defences where waves battered our shores. They marched right up and down the entire British Isles, growling like minotaurs.

Cables were dashed down as the storms rampaged and roared. Whole forests were torn into matchsticks. Everyone hid indoors. Except for where we lived. We still had to go to school . . .

"*This storm is pretty bad!*" my friend Bod's mother yelled from the canteen kitchen.

"I don't think it's *too* bad!" cried Mr Flopp, our Head Teacher. "It could all blow past soon." (Fat chance; it was here to stay.)

"I think we should go home —"

"No, we can stick it out!" (Mr Flopp's crazy.)

The whole school was cowering under quaking desks and our teacher, Miss Baboon, was shrieking like a bat. Meanwhile Mr Flopp walked around, shouting, "It's not that bad!"

(See? He *is* crazy.)

"We can wait till lunchtime —"

What for, to be sick? Our school was bouncing round like flotsam on the sea. It's a really old place which practically falls apart if someone sneezes.

"There are no potatoes!" I heard Bod's mother cry.

"Well, give them something else!" Mr Flopp bellowed back.

"I don't cook anything else."

"Just give them peas and meat."

"The butcher hasn't come . . ."

If I'm going to be honest, though, food wasn't our main concern. Our main concern was our school roof, which simply blew away while we were sitting there reading the blackboard.

"*It's an emergency!*" Miss Baboon shrieked, as all our books and things were blown about like autumn leaves. She dived to the floor like she was about to say her prayers. "Everyone's going to die!"

"Don't be so brainless," said our Head. (He's very hard.) "Has anyone brought a canvas sheet to school?" he asked.

What kind of a question is that? We had a pencil case, two marbles, one dead rat . . .

"I've got some knickers," Bod's mum said from the hall.

"*What?*" Mr Flopp's eyes bulged, like balloons about to burst.

"I keep a pair handy for emergencies. I've got them in my bag."

Bod's mum started groping inside her enormous bag, but Mr Flopp yelled, "No! Please leave them where they are!"

"But we could hoist them up as a temporary roof. They'd keep the rain out."

Mr Flopp staggered backwards like someone about to swoon. "This can't be real!" he gasped. "This isn't happening. You want to hoist your knickers up for a new school roof?"

"Just till the repair man comes."

Chapter 3

I don't mind telling you that it took us quite a while to haul those knickers up.

They were stupendous – they almost swamped the school. I don't know how Bod's mum got them into her bag. It was like a magic box which let whole worlds tumble out when you opened it.

It took the whole school to get them into

shape, boys pulling from the halls, girls climbing up the walls. While the rain came pouring in, and Miss Baboon fainted, Bod's mum cried, "Here we go!"

Using some thick ropes which were kept under the stairs, we stretched the knickers out, spreading them on the floor. Our panting Head Teacher looked round. "We need a volunteer to tie these to the beams. Ah, Miss Baboon!" he said. "Is that you hiding there?"

Our skinny teacher had recovered from fainting and was taking refuge behind Bod. Her face was twisted with anxiety and her glasses had slipped off.

"I'm not too agile —"

"Nonsense! You'll do just fine." Mr Flopp yanked her out and forced her on to a chair. "Just climb on to my back, then up on my shoulders . . ." We had to shove her up.

"I'm not too stable!" she squealed, as Mr

Flopp staggered around the room, bending beneath her weight.

"Steady on!" he cried, and breathed in startled chokes as her legs locked round his throat.

"Okay, I've got it now," he croaked, as he pushed Miss Baboon up.

She hung on like a bat and reached down for the rope.

"Grip one end in your teeth. You'll need to use both hands to balance on those beams," said Mr Flopp.

"I'm getting vertigo!" yelled Miss Baboon.

The next half hour was pandemonium. By the end of it Mr Flopp had a black eye and Miss Baboon was hanging upside down.

"Have you got those drawers up yet?" Mr Flopp's voice cried out from somewhere in the folds of the knickers. "I'm starting to suffocate —"

"My nose is in the knot!"

"I've found a bag of sprouts!" I heard Bod's mother cry. "We can have sprouts and peas!"

Oh, wow! I'll really enjoy school dinner this time, you guys.

"Have you tied that knot yet?"

"Well, I've got something tied."

"Then tie the other end!"

We all watched, open-mouthed. It was amazing to see somebody so puny fling themselves around in that way.

"I think I've nailed it!" we heard Miss Baboon cry.

"Then come back down to earth."

"I'm coming down!" she yelled.
The entire school stood back
to watch Bod's mum's
knickers hold the
wind and rain
at bay.

Chapter 4

"What was that creaking sound?" Miss Baboon mused aloud, halfway through her lesson.

We all looked up. The knickers were still in place.

We stared down at the floor. What *was* that creaking sound?

"The whole school's taking off!" I heard

somebody cry from the classroom next door.

We charged for the windows, Miss Baboon to the fore. "Oh, no!" her thin voice howled. "The school's in the air!" (If you want *tough* knickers, ask Bod's mother where to get them.)

To our astonishment, the earth had dropped away. The wind had filled those knickers like an old ship's mighty sail, and we were soaring like a bird (except a normal bird would know which way was up!)

The school was swinging around like a drunken ape. Schoolkids bounced off the walls – I ended up on top of Bod. He just said, "Get off my chest, please." (He's a placid boy who takes things in his stride.)

"Everyone to the guy ropes!" Bod's mother yelled. "We'll have to shed some sail!"

You what? We're in a school . . .

"Make way! Make way!" she cried, forcing her vast bulk through, pinging us off like peas.

It was Bod's courageous mum who stayed out in the school yard, braving the wind and rain, stray seagulls and passing clouds. It was Bod's fearless mum who, guy ropes in each hand, forced our school back on course.

She looked magnificent as she jeered at the storm. "*Storm, do your worst!*" she cried, her sleeves pushed up her arms. Her laughter filled the school, and we yelled back as one, "Yeah, yeah! Go, go, Bod's mum!"

Chapter 5

Frimley school sailed through the air like a vast hot air balloon, with Bod's mother in control.

As she grew more confident she began to try some tricks, shouting, *"Wha-hoah! Wha-hey!"* as the school looped the loop. I gripped on to Bod's legs as we turned upside down, and Mr Flopp shot past us.

We were caught up in the storm, and it swept us far from land as night began to fall.

Mr Flopp gathered us together in the school canteen.

"As you probably all know," he said portentously, "we are now in the air, high over the North Sea. Thanks to Bod's mother we're on an even keel and in no immediate danger. We are, however, helpless in the storm, with no idea of where we're heading for. It could be John o' Groats. It could be the Isle of Man. It could be Iceland.

"In order to keep our spirits up, in this our darkest hour, I think now is the time to sing the old school song. . ."

We met him with blank stares. Our school doesn't *have* a song.

". . . which I have just written."

We all sat patiently while he took his notebook out and held it at arm's length so that he could read the words.

Wedging his glasses tightly on his nose, he said in a sombre voice, "Repeat after me:

"Here we go, here we go, here we go.
Zooming up, soaring high, swooping loo-ow.
Like a moth, or a sky filled with crows,
Here we go-o, here we go . . .

"Verse Two!" he yelled.

"Here we go, here we go, here we go,
Here we go, here we go, here we go-o . . ."

So we sang, and we stamped, and we danced.
    "Here we go-o, here we go . . ."

27

Just after midnight – it was pitch black outside – Bod's hand shook me awake.

"I think we're landing."

"Where are we coming down?"

"Who knows?" Bod whispered. "We're over glaciers —"

"It could be Iceland, then."

"Well, it isn't Huddersfield."

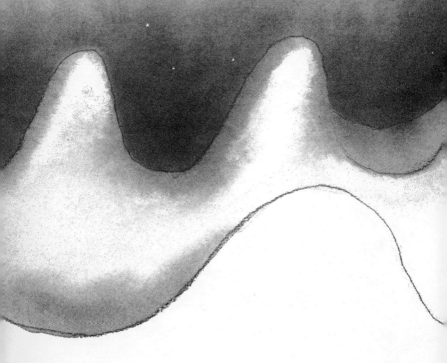

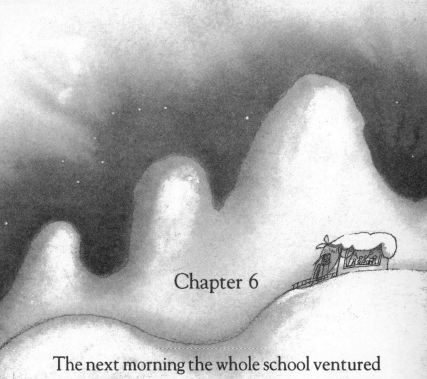

Chapter 6

The next morning the whole school ventured out into the white landscape which now surrounded us.

With the weather being so cold that we might freeze to death, we'd pulled Bod's mum's knickers down from the school roof and wrapped them round ourselves. Mr Flopp tried to start a fire to warm us up, but

set his tie alight. He started howling as flames crept up his chest, but Bod's mum bashed them out with an iron frying pan.

"Thanks very much," he croaked, as she then pulled him up and dusted down his clothes.

Then we crept forward like a giant centipede, with our thin, white legs poking down in the snow.

We hadn't got as far as the school gate when Miss Baboon went mad and galloped off, shrieking.

"She's gone snow-crazy!" Mr Flopp bellowed, as spindly-legged Miss Baboon high-tailed it through the yard. "Somebody save her!"

We all went tearing off, trying to bring her down before she did herself some damage.

"Stand aside!" bellowed Bod's mum, making up a snowball and weighing it in her hand. "I used to enjoy this."

She pulled her right arm back, and hurled the snowball. Miss Baboon crashed to the ground as it bounced off her skull.

"My word! Is she all right?" asked a startled Mr Flopp. "Try throwing another."

We all looked puzzled, and he added hastily, "Such a good shot. Was that a fluke, or can she really be that good? Could she play on the team when we take on the staff of Cranbourne Cricket School?"

While we debated this point Miss Baboon scrambled up, and stumbled round the yard, before falling again. In a weak voice she cried, "Was that a grizzly bear?"

"It's our new fast bowler!" we yelled.

Chapter 7

We left our school behind and set off on a search for food or rescue.

We didn't find either. All we did find was a gorge which plummeted straight down a thousand metres or more. Far below we could see tiny dots, like ink-stains on the snow, which might have been houses.

"Look, sir, a rope-bridge!" cried Bod,

pointing to a frost-encrusted rope which snaked across the gorge. It looked an ideal way for us to kill ourselves . . .

"Don't fancy that," I growled.

We needed someone courageous to brave the gorge and go in search of help.

We looked at Mr Flopp, but his gaze was elsewhere.

"Ah, Miss Baboon . . ." he smiled.

"I don't really like this much," bleated poor

Miss Baboon, as she swung from the rope.

"Nonsense! You'll be fine," cried Mr Flopp. "Keep staring straight ahead, and don't look down at all. At least the power cables will kill you long before you ever hit the ground!"

Miss Baboon looked nervous. "Power cables?" she whimpered.

"Just my little joke. Ha ha!" our Head replied. "They're not real power cables – just steel girders on that bridge far below."

That seemed to calm Miss Baboon, and she began to lurch across the gorge, clinging with hands and heels to the thin rope. Her skirt blew in her eyes, but she could see okay by peering down her legs.

"It's a very long way!" she cried.

"Nonsense! You're almost there," shouted back Mr Flopp.

What kind of a lie was that? She had hardly started.

Bod's mother mopped her brow, and paced around in the snow, muttering worriedly.

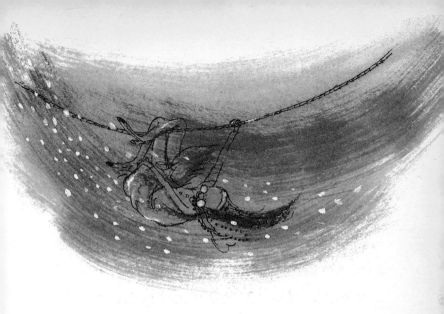

Chapter 8

We watched with open mouths as plucky Miss Baboon crept out across the gorge.

We shouted encouraging remarks, like, *"We can see your knickers!"* Which in fact we couldn't, because she was facing the wrong way. But it still made us laugh to watch her try to tuck her skirt into her shoes.

She was halfway across when a storm

swept in, with snowflakes as big as clouds. They swirled around her head and covered up her eyes.

"I think she's frozen!"

Miss Baboon didn't move as the storm raged all around and snow settled on her head. It was left to Bod's brave mum to say, "Stand clear, you lot! I'm going to bring her in!"

She grabbed the frail rope, which made poor Miss Baboon go bouncing up and down like a fly caught in a web. But she was frozen fast, and could do little more than shout, "It's cold out here!"

With her apron flapping, Bod's mum went swinging out, inching across the gorge with both hands clinging tight. The rope gave an ominous creak, and Mr Flopp cried out, "Quick! Make sure it's secure!"

But as we all rushed forward to check the flimsy knot, it parted with a twang, and the whole rope hurtled down. Bod's mum cried, "*Flipping heck! Wah-hey!*" as she swung down towards the other side of the gorge . . .

We watched with wide eyes as she crashed into the ice, punching a perfect hole out as she thundered through.

A little way above her head, a startled Miss Baboon was still clinging on to the rope.

Chapter 9

Ten minutes after that we found a bridge across the gorge and dug out Bod's poor mum.

We also pulled Miss Baboon up and dried her by a fire, watching as clouds of steam rose up from her. "Of all the things I've done in my life . . ." she began.

"What?"

"That was one of them."

Then we stoked up the fire, using some chopped-up desks that we'd brought from the school. Huddled against the chill, surrounded by snowy wastes, we toasted icicles.

But even the windbreak which Bod's mum's knickers provided couldn't keep out all the draughts, and the wild wind whistled through. It whipped up red sparks, and they settled on Mr Flopp, setting his hair alight . . .

Bod watched me, puzzled. "Did you hear that?" he said.

I looked back. "Did I hear what?" I asked.

"That singing on the breeze."

"What singing on the breeze?"

"*Hi ho, hi ho,*" he said.

I was a bit distracted, because I was watching Mr Flopp tearing around in the snow, smoke pouring from his head. Bod's mum saved him again, using her frying pan to club him to the ground.

"Do you think she's killed him?" I asked.

"She's beating out the flames. But never mind that now," Bod went on, "what about that strange song?"

"The *Hi ho, hi ho* song?"

"Exactly."

"Yes, I heard it."

"So who was singing it?"

I'd thought that Bod was, so now I looked around and saw a group of men dressed in farming gear. They were marching straight for us, singing, "*Hi ho, hi ho,*" in a fairly tuneless way.

"Norwegian farmers," Bod muttered

knowingly. "In the distinctive garb of farmers of that ilk."

"What?"

"Don't you read? It was in *Distinctive Garbs*."

"I never got that far."

The Norwegian farmers, their apple-rosy cheeks glowing, came marching up to us.

"Good morning, campers!" The first one gave a smile.

"Good morning," we replied, "oh farmers of that ilk."

"You what?"

"It's in *Distinctive Garbs*."

The farmer looked puzzled. "We never got

that far." He glanced around him. "You haven't seen our cows?"

We turned our pockets out, and said, "No cows in here."

"That's too bad," he replied, gazing off through the storm and stroking his smooth white chin.

"What do they look like?" Bod's mum said helpfully.

"They look like any cows you'd find in a storm. What kind of question's that?"

"I'm only trying to help."

"Well, don't," the farmer growled.

Suddenly he went crazy, crying, "Enough of this! I'm tired of tramping around, pretending we've lost some cows! It's time to show our hand!" And he ripped off his wig and all his farmer's clothes.

It was very dramatic, because it all came off as one, and underneath we saw a completely new person. Instead of Farmer

Klaus, your friendly milk farmer, we saw – bandits!

"Good grief! Bandits!" exploded Mr Flopp, as one after another the men pulled off their farmers' garb.

Standing before our eyes, bristling with knives and ropes, were gaucho bandits!

"Ha ha! A mighty change, no?" demanded their leader. "No more the stinking pigs who run around after cows!" He had a big moustache and a wild shock of black hair. "Moo moo – no more!" he cried.

We staggered backwards, amazed at what we saw. Miss Baboon went down and we all tripped over her. Bod's mother fell on top of us all, murmuring, "Well, bless my soul! Who would have dreamed it?"

Chapter 10

We sat around in the snow while all the bandits fought for possession of the gun. They only had one, which they were supposed to hold in turn, but the biggest of them all had decided it was his. He had the biggest hat and the biggest black moustache. His nose was bigger too.

"I am Alfredo, and I'm the boss!" he cried,

knocking the whole lot flat with one sweep of his hand. They scrambled up again and leapt on to his back, kicking out furiously.

"I am Alfredo!" we heard him croaking, and every now and then he waved the gun around.

There wasn't much for us to do, so we played gin rummy with a pack of cards Bod's mother had brought along.

At last the fight died down and a voice said, "Why don't you pick up that jack there?"

Our eyes glanced upwards, to meet Alfredo's gaze.

"Do you mind? We're playing cards."

"I know! I know!" he cried. "I was just trying to help!"

"Well, don't."

"That's it!" he yelled. "I'm going to shoot you all!"

He took his gun out and waved it furiously, and then it went off, startling a passing duck, which plunged down in the snow, checked itself for holes, then flapped away again.

"That was just a warning. Next time it is for real."

The duck flew back again. "What?"

"Next time it's for real."

"Okay." The duck flew off.

Bod and I looked around. What kind of a place was this?

Chapter 11

Alfredo di Fredo, the deadly bandit, spoke from the top of a mound of snow. His hat was pushed back on his greasy head. His thumbs were hooked in his belt, which was hung with evil-looking knives. His cohorts gathered around him, brandishing chair and table legs in place of guns.

"I am Alfredo the Assassin!" he cried.

"Who have you killed lately?"

"No one. I'm new to the job. But we are fierce bandits, sent on a deadly mission to kidnap Norway!"

He paused dramatically, while we all looked around.

"I *said* it was Norway!"

"You said it was Hartlepool!"

"Silence!" Alfredo cried. "I am the man in charge. I say what's Hartlepool."

He took a step back and tumbled from the mound, and when he crawled back up his hat was over his eyes. "Who killed the lights?" he croaked.

"It's your hat," we replied.

"That's it! The hat must die!"

"Now listen here, my man," spoke up our gallant Head, who'd done a nifty clothes swap with Miss Baboon, "I am a young woman, and I've a right to know what's going on around here."

Alfredo grunted. "A very fine young woman. But what happened to your hair? It looks all singed on top. However, you are right to ask, and I am about to say. Stop interrupting me."

He took a deep breath and went on, "You will all know that South America is quite a hilly place, except in Uruguay, where we have little hills, no more than grass pimples.

This is a great loss to sporty types like us, so we hatched up a plan to claim hills of our own. In fact, forget the hills – we thought we'd steal a mountain range, complete with snow-capped peaks!"

Alfredo's excitement grew as he began to describe his plan, which involved planting explosive charges at the head of the Hardanger Fjord.

"We'll steal their mountains!"

Alfredo's men went wild.

"Sail them across the sea and up the River Plate!"

The bandits cheered like mad. Even Bod's mum joined in.

"THEN WE'LL HAVE WINTER SPORTS!"

Chapter 12

Bod and I trudged along, a rope across our backs, muttering under our breath.

The great Alfredo had gone and lost his sledges, with all his dogs and half of his supplies, so he'd commandeered our school and was making us pull it along like a pack of huskies.

We were straining to get the school across

a great glacier and now Alfredo was cracking a big whip, shouting, "Mush, mush, you pigs!" as we struggled along.

You know, as school trips go, this was almost the worst we had ever been on.

"I'm knackered!" Bod said, as we slumped down for our lunchtime rest. We were eating snowflakes mixed with wood chips, which tasted quite a lot like Bod's mum's pease pudding. She'd tried to tart it up by dotting lumps of snow over the gritty parts.

"What we could do with is some kind of plan," I said.

"Like rigging my mum's knickers up as a sail?" Bod suggested.

"That sounds okay."

"I thought it was," said Bod. "Go and tell Alfredo."

Chapter 13

With the knickers tied in place between a flagpole and a wall we skimmed across the ground in the school, cheering as the ice passed beneath us. Bod's mum was steering us as she had done before. She didn't do any loop-the-loops this time, though once or twice she tried some fancy pirouettes.

It was all plain sailing, or so we believed,

until a gaping gorge opened up in our path. We were going flat out and there would be little chance of pulling up in time.

"*Somebody save us!*" bellowed Miss Baboon. "You are the man in charge!" she cried out to Alfredo, grabbing him by the throat and shaking him. "Come on! Do something!"

Alfredo reeled back. "Get this man off me!"

"I'm just wearing men's clothes. I'm only a helpless girl."

"Not so helpless," he groaned. "You're almost choking me." His face turned red and green.

"I know the answer!" Bod's mum cried suddenly. "Find a length of rope, and tie it round my waist."

With the rope fixed in place she then jumped over the school gate like a vast anchor, and dug her heels in, sending up clouds of snow.

"*Wha-hoah! Wha-hey!*" she cried. It looked like touch and go, but she was tugging hard to slow the school down.

We pulled up on the very edge of the gorge, with Bod's mum buried deep inside a mound of snow.

Chapter 14

Nobody dared to move as we hung on the edge of a great, yawning pit. The drop seemed endless.

"No one move," Alfredo murmured. "And the fattest ones should move the least of all. Who is the fattest one? Chuck that boy over the edge!"

Billy Green started to cry.

At that moment, the school began to move again, and we saw Bod's brave mum trudging across the ice. Completely covered in snow, she ploughed blindly ahead like a great juggernaut.

We heard the creaking of the rope and grunting from Bod's mum. We shared in every step she took. She pulled us away from the edge and then, as darkness fell, crashed down into the snow.

Chapter 15

The next day we had to abandon our school when it froze to the ground and continue our way on foot.

Following barren trails we wound past raging falls, all the while heading up towards high, snow-capped peaks. There white-tailed eagles soared and ibex leapt like elves through the clouds.

Our only guide now was a map Alfredo had, which seemed strangely at odds with the terrain we were walking. It was left to Miss Baboon to work out that it was a map of Scotland.

"This isn't Scotland —"

"I know, I got confused." Alfredo scratched his head. "So many maps to choose from. But this one was half-price, so I thought, Oh what the heck? It's got mountains on it."

"They're not the same ones —"

"Oh, they're all much the same." Alfredo crumpled up the map, and pushed it into his coat. "We don't need maps, really; I've got a brilliant nose for sniffing out a route."

He raised one finger, as if testing the air. Then he checked a broken nail and tutted, "Look at that! It really does your nails in, being a bandit – stripping down guns and things.

"I'm nearly starved to death," he grunted, changing the subject. "We should look for some food before we all collapse. There must be fish round here, with all these streams and things. Who's got a fishing rod?"

We didn't have one, although we found a stream heaving with salmon fins. All we now needed was someone with brains, but we were low on brains – we just had bandits.

"Let's jump in and catch them with our hands!" one of them exclaimed.

"You fool!" Alfredo snarled. He pondered

a while, then went on. "We *could* do that. I've seen brown bears do it on the wildlife programmes, and they are only bears, while we're crack bandits! We can out-fish a bear!"

So in great excitement we lined up on the bank, watching the rushing stream in which our dinner lurked.

"Go up the stream and chase the fish this way," Alfredo ordered his men.

"That water's freezing!" one of them pointed out.

"What are you, mice or men?" Alfredo pushed them in. "Don't be such feeble types. You've got the easy part!"

Chapter 16

We stood with bated breath as the grim bandits came wading up the stream, hurling rocks into the water to drive the fish into our waiting arms. We were all poised to pounce.

"There's one!" cried Miss Baboon, thwacking a mallard.

"That's not a salmon," Mr Flopp said patiently. "What you've stunned is a

67

duck – a mallard duck."

"Sorry, I got confused." Miss Baboon turned bright pink. "The thrill of the hunt took me over."

Then someone cried, "They're coming up the stream!"

All eyes turned to observe the grey, speeding dorsal fins. They were heading our way, sending up veils of spray, cutting the waves like knives.

"Get ready, Frimley!" Mr Flopp bellowed. "We'll only get one chance, so make sure it counts!"

"I've got my saucepan out!" yelled Bod's mum from the rear. "I'll get the fire going!"

The fish tore up the stream while we lumbered about trying to pick them up.

We were knocked over backwards and crashed into the stream. We caught fish in our arms and they sprang out again. I grabbed Mr Flopp's leg (though quite by accident) and ducked him upside down.

"I think I've got one!" Miss Baboon cried joyfully, though when she pulled it out it was only her foot. It was quite like a fish – you could see why she thought she'd caught a big salmon.

But amidst all the confusion the fish were swimming past, and it would not be long before our chance had gone.

"Stand back – I'm coming through!" Bod's mother yelled at last, as she charged for the stream.

Casting her vast knickers like a great swirling net, she trapped a dozen fish inside the thick white folds. Then she began lashing out with her huge frying pan, trying to stun them.

"I think I've got them!"

We all dived in to help, but somehow those fish seemed quite well organized. By swimming as a team they got the net to move, and hurtled off downstream.

"Watch out! Don't lose them!" Bod's mum gave a great leap and grabbed the trailing edge of her speeding knickers. "Relax, I'm in control!"

But Bod's mum spoke too soon, for the fish were pulling hard.

They dragged her under. "*Wha-hoah!*" Bod's mother yelled.

"*Yah-hey!*" she cried again as her round head bobbed back up.

We all covered our eyes as the net reached the edge of a high waterfall.

Chapter 17

Bod's mum's knickers snagged on the edge of a forbidding drop, which crashed in foam and roars.

"I'll save you!" Mr Flopp shouted, galloping through the stream like a charging windmill. "I'll hold on to your legs!"

"Be quick – I'm going down!"

"No, no!" our Head shrieked.

Bod's mum slipped out of sight and Mr Flopp took off with a despairing lunge . . .

Mr Flopp ground his teeth as Bod's mum swung upside down, held by her ankles.

We heard his bones creaking as he clung on desperately.

"Quick! Someone toss a line!" he cried.

We threw a ball of string.

"No, toss a *thicker* line!" Someone flung a rope, and Mr Flopp clutched it.

He tied a sheep-shank, although there were no sheep in sight. "Now pull me in!" he cried, and we pulled him in, crying out with joy as Bod's mum's head appeared above the raging falls.

"I've got the net!" she yelled triumphantly, grabbing Mr Flopp's nose as she clambered from the falls.

We all smelled fish for tea, except for Mr Flopp, whose nose was bandaged up.

Chapter 18

The next morning we climbed a high cliff, fell down the other side, then scaled another one.

We climbed up so high we were above the clouds, and our school far below was just a tiny dot. You could have picked it up and wiped it on your sleeve, then plonked it down again.

We seemed so helpless, wandering through the snow, and I began to fear we wouldn't last for long . . . I might have shed a tear, but someone else had cried and got their eyes iced up.

Alfredo pointed to his map. "Which part is this?" he asked.

"That's the north of Scotland."

That seemed to please him. "That's close enough," he said. "They have got mountains too, and they're the same as these. Tomorrow they'll be ours, sailing across the sea towards the River Plate."

I saw a problem. "Norway will want them back," I said.

"Norway will never know it was us who took them. We'll leave a note behind, saying the land-nappers were not from Uruguay." Alfredo folded the map up. "No problems now," he finished.

"What's that strange rumbling sound?"
said Bod's mum.

We gazed towards the peaks and saw a wall
of snow thundering down on us.

"Watch out! Don't panic!"
Why not? I'm good at that.

We took off down that slope like we were chased by eels. We went down slithering, galloping, hurtling, and kicking up veils of snow.

With every moment the avalanche closed in, making the mountain shake, throwing up plumes of ice. We'd never get away before that roaring wall came crashing over us.

"Everyone – jump on this!"

It was Bod's mum's knickers, which she'd

thrown down on the ground. We quickly jumped aboard and sailed off like a sledge. The wind beat in our eyes, ice crystals stung our cheeks, but we stayed out ahead.

The only problem was when we reached the edge of a gorge and shot off into space like a great dying swan.

I don't know who screamed the most, Mr Flopp or Miss Baboon. Bod's mum just yelled, "*Wha-hey! Wha-hey!*"

We spiralled down to earth and landed in a heap, Bod's mum on top of us.

How does she *do* this? She does it every time. Bod's mum just has a way of coming out on top.

I couldn't ask her then because the avalanche was pouring down on us.

In order to escape it we dived into a cave, and blocked the entrance up with Bod's mum's thick knickers.

They kept the snow at bay while we huddled for warmth round our last matchstick.

Chapter 19

Next day we faced the final leg of our hazardous trek.

It was all downhill to the Hardanger Fjord, through fields of knee-high grass, bunnies and grazing cows. Glaciers disappeared as we trotted along, singing the new school song.

But our excitement was doomed to be short-lived. Alfredo di Fredo had no room for us in his plans.

"All witnesses will have to be removed," he announced. "Sorry, that's how it is."

We stared in horror. "You can't mean us!" we cried.

Alfredo shrugged his shoulders. "There's no one else round here."

"What are you going to do?"

"I'm going to tie you up and throw you in the fjord."

Some kind of friend he is! I'd thought he was fond of us.

Never trust a bandit.

Chapter 20

We watched the wild bandits abseiling down the side of the fjord to plant their charges in the cliffside.

They were packing explosives into cracks in the rock, intending to fracture off a whole chunk of Norway. Then they would sail it home, using a big outboard motor they'd brought along with them.

It sounded crazy, but then you never know – people do crazy things and get away with them. Bod's mother had saved our school and brought us to Norway . . .

(Where was Bod's mum, by the way?)

"Okay," Alfredo said, "there's fifteen minutes to go, then it's all over. The bombs will go off and we will sail back home, and this whole mountain range will belong to Uruguay. You've all been very nice, but we can't take you along. Go find your own mountains."

Then he started sniggering. "But since you're all tied up, you won't find anything except fish in the sea! Hah hah! What do you think of that? A pretty evil plan, I think you must agree!"

Everyone nodded. Yes, that's an evil plan. It takes a real bandit to think up plans like that. The best plan I could think up was quite

impractical. We had no guillotines.

"While we are waiting," Alfredo rambled on, "I thought it might be nice to tell you my life story. If you are going to die, then you should know the man who makes it possible."

"Are we supposed to take notes?" Miss Baboon piped up.

Alfredo frowned in thought, then said, "A good idea. José! Go find some pens, and pass them round the group. Loosen their bonds slightly."

We started scribbling as Alfredo stood up and began pacing up and down, his thumbs tucked in his belt. His thoughts were far away, back in his childhood . . .

Chapter 21

"When I was a little boy I grew up very poor, inside a poor family. My father, Santos – he was a poor, poor man. Mama Victoria – she was a poor one too. On my grandmother's side —"

"Does this go on for long?"

"Shut up!" Alfredo snarled.

He continued in his droning voice, "I had a

85

little dog, a little tiny pooch, whose name was Cheeky-Poo. We had to sell that dog to buy ourselves some food – that is how poor we were!"

He started howling. "I really miss that dog! I miss his little tongue licking my small, damp hand. I miss his little nose, his thin tail wagging. *Mama – I loved that dog!*"

We looked around us, but his mama wasn't there. There was no one but Frimley School and a crowd of bawling bandits. They were all weeping as they listened to Alfredo's

tale, so we passed hankies around.

"And then my black cat – *she went and sold my cat!*"

(This was a sordid tale of a betrayed childhood. I knew it could go on for hours. I'd better skip the rest.)

Alfredo checked the time. "Only five minutes left. You'd better come and watch."

We all marched forward to see the great display of desperado crime and the looting of Norway. Together we gazed down on the cliffs which, in five minutes' time, would be blasted apart.

"There goes Bod's mother!" I heard somebody cry. Craning out to look, I saw her far below. She was descending the cliff, her knickers in her hand.

"She's got her knickers with her!"

We started cheering and waving Bod's brave mum on.

Alfredo gave a snort. "She won't get there in time. Only four minutes left."

"Four minutes!" we cried.

Bod's mum waved in reply.

Alfredo filed his nails with an air of unconcern, as Bod's mum scaled the cliff.

"She'll never make it. Those are the very best – the finest bombs there are, complete with guarantees. I got them from that shop just outside San José. The brand new superstore."

He checked his wristwatch.

"Forty-five seconds left."

Bod's mum stopped for a rest and took a sandwich out of her bag.

"Not now! Not now!" we cried. "You've got to save Norway! The world depends on you!"

She crammed the sandwich back, picked up her big handbag and continued down the cliff.

"Twenty-five seconds left."

She reached the cache of bombs.

"Fifteen – *fourteen* seconds."

"Just fourteen seconds left!"

Bod's mum waved cheerily.

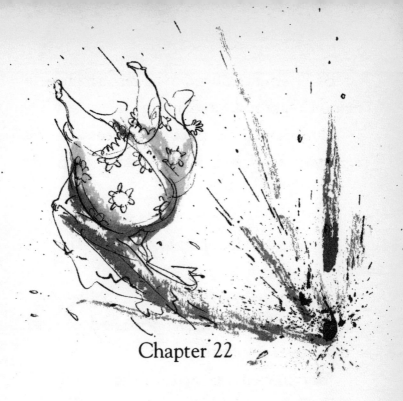

Chapter 22

Bod's mum folded her knickers and placed them on top of the bombs, then gingerly sat down on them. As the last seconds ticked by, she took a pen from her bag and began to fill a crossword in. She was bent over the page filling in Four Down when the bombs blew up.

Bod's mum looked startled as she began to

rock, then she rose into the air, gripping the singed cloth. The knickers absorbed the blast, but sent her rocketing towards the distant sky. Her eyes grew wide as she passed through the clouds, and then plunged down again.

It was touch and go, but at last the knickers filled out to leave her drifting down like a vast hang-glider. The school let out a cheer as Bod's mum looped the loop with carefree nonchalance.

Only Alfredo seemed less than overjoyed. "That does it!" he growled. "I want my money back! Those bombs are second-rate!"

Chapter 23

The Norwegian police arrived, to see what was happening, and Alfredo's gang ran off.

We were carried into town aboard a golden sled, like heroes. Bod's mum stood at the front, handing out autographs.

Her scorched knickers became the town's new flag, and will hang for ever more above the Town Hall steps.

Our school was left behind, but a new one was soon built. This time the roof is welded on!

94